FIVE GO
GLUTEN FREE

Other adventures in this series:

Five Go Parenting
Five Go on a Strategy Away Day
Five on Brexit Island
Five Give Up the Booze

Enid Blyton

FIVE GO GLUTEN FREE

Text by
Bruno Vincent

Enid Blyton for Grown-Ups

Quercus

First published in Great Britain in 2016 by

Quercus Editions Ltd
Carmelite House
50 Victoria Embankment
London EC4Y 0DZ

An Hachette UK company

A CIP catalogue record for this book is available
from the British Library

HB ISBN 978 1 78648 222 8
EBOOK ISBN 978 1 78648 223 5

Text by Bruno Vincent
Original illustrations by Eileen A. Soper
Cover illustration by Ruth Palmer

17

Typeset by CC Book Production

Printed and bound in Australia by McPhersons Printing Group

Contents

1 A LOVELY BIRTHDAY PICNIC   1

2 A FIRM RESOLUTION   5

3 A SURPRISING HEALTH SPECIALIST   11

4 THE NEW REGIME   20

5 PLANNING AHEAD   23

6 THE FIRST WEEK   28

7 TIME FOR A CHANGE   35

8 THE JOURNEY, NOT THE DESTINATION   39

9 A SURPRISE ABOUT KIRRIN ISLAND   45

10 'FREE-FROM' EVERYTHING AT
    KIRRIN COTTAGE   54

11 GETTING TO KNOW DORSET AGAIN   58

12 A CYCLING ADVENTURE   67

13 THINGS COME TO A HEAD   78

14 THE RIDE HOME IS INTERRUPTED   85

15 EXTRA-SPECIAL GUESTS   91

16 A BRISK JOURNEY HOME   101

CHAPTER ONE

A Lovely Birthday Picnic

It was a beautiful sunny afternoon in early summer and Julian, George, Dick and Anne had decided to go for a picnic in the park. Timmy was nearby, leaping around in pursuit of butterflies, barking, and generally looking like he was having a jolly time.

'Oh, you are all *so* wonderful,' Anne was saying. She was sitting surrounded by wrapping paper and clutching a cookery book to her chest, for they had gathered at the picnic to celebrate her birthday. 'Dick, you are just the *sweetest*,' she said.

'Not at all, dear Anne,' said Dick. 'There's no present that's good enough for you!'

(George silently marvelled that, as a grown man, Dick never got tired of these saccharine goings-on, but, seeing as the supply of cream buns was still plentiful, she was happy to keep her thoughts to herself for the time being.)

'No present good enough, that is,' said Julian with a complacent smile, 'except, perhaps, this one.'

1

He handed over a card, which Anne duly ripped open with a total lack of girlish decorum. She read the slip of paper that fell out of it, and squeaked.

'Oh, Julian,' she said. 'I've run out of superlatives. A weekend at a well-being retreat! For me and a plus one.'

'You should take one of your girl chums,' said Julian.

'Perhaps George would like it?' added Dick, watching George carefully.

'Huh,' grunted George. 'If they serve lager I could sit in the bar and watch the rugby, I suppose.'

Anne laughed, threw the card down and gave Julian a big hug. 'Obviously I wouldn't insult George by asking her,' she said, sitting back and smoothing her dress out prettily. 'One of the girls from Bikram yoga will go with me.'

'Last but not least . . .' said George, handing over a box topped with a fat-ribboned bow.

Anne let out an even higher-pitched squeak than before and the other three all winced. Twenty yards away, Timmy looked round. Anne fell on the wrapping like a hungry lion upon an overweight antelope, and then sat back, looking at the box and wondering what to make of it.

'What do you want to give her a mangle for?' asked Julian.

Anne, never able to bear any conflict (and most especially not at her birthday celebrations), opened her mouth to say a

'A spiralizer!' Anne let out a high-pitched squeal of delight.

mangle was a most *thoughtful* present. But she was interrupted by Dick.

'It's not a mangle, Julian,' he said. 'It's a pasta maker.'

'Oh, *George*,' said Anne.

'For pity's sake, just read the box,' said George impatiently. 'It's neither of those things. It's a spiralizer.'

A low moan of realization went up around the picnic blanket, followed by a brief silence.

'What's a spiralizer?' asked Anne. 'Darling George,' she added quickly.

'Read the box,' George repeated.

Anne did so, with mounting fascination. Then, remembering herself, she gave George a great big hug. She spent the next hour reading not only the instruction manual, but the cookery book Dick had given her, cooing occasionally at interesting-sounding ingredients, like chia seeds and goji berries, and attempting to engage the interest of the others in what she was reading.

Soon it was time to pack up and go home, but not before Anne had given everyone a kiss for what she described as 'the best birthday picnic a girl ever had!'

CHAPTER TWO

A Firm Resolution

Anne was so taken with her presents that she read the cookbook all the way home and then immediately prepared dinner using the spiralizer.

Although Anne always did the cooking for the group, her dear brothers and cousin had refused to allow her to prepare the food for her own birthday picnic. George had made a loaf of banana bread, Dick some biscuits and Julian had tried his hand at a tart. Because they cooked so rarely, however, this had resulted in a marked drop-off in quality from the picnics they usually enjoyed, meaning most of the food had been left uneaten and they were all now famished. And, seeing as Anne's actual birthday had been the previous Thursday, they had no compunctions about allowing her to cook their evening meal.

Thus, come supper time, they were somewhat surprised to be presented with a very pale, spaghetti-like substance, which proved extremely soft to the touch of a fork. Hardly daring, quite yet, to question her, they waited while Anne presently piled roasted vegetables on each of their plates, poured them a glass of something odd and cloudy, and then sat to eat her own.

'Looks fascinating,' said Dick quietly.

'Looks . . . jolly *interesting*, at least,' said Julian.

'What the hell is this?' asked George.

Although it might seem a slightly ungrateful response, in a certain manner George's question was a fair one. Ever since moving in together, their evening meals had been served according to an unwavering schedule: spaghetti Bolognese on Mondays and Thursdays, shepherd's pie on Tuesdays, baked potatoes on Wednesdays and fish pie on Fridays. It was a plan of Anne's origination, because she made all the food. She stuck rigidly to this cooking rota, which was why George questioned the plate of pale noodles in front of her.

'The drink is magic water,' said Anne.

'*Magic* water?' asked Julian. 'Don't tell me you've exchanged our only cow for *this*?'

'Very funny, Julian,' said Anne. 'It's a revitalizing health drink that contains ginger, leaves, fruit juices. The food is called "courgetti".' Then, as Dick opened his mouth, she added, 'That's spaghetti made from courgette. It tastes just like the real thing – I promise, you won't notice the difference!'

'So we're having starters now?' asked George. 'That's really pushing the boat out, Anne.'

Anne cleared her throat and smiled at everyone. 'No, this is all we're having.'

The other three looked at each other, and then eventually back to Anne.

'Anne?' asked Julian. 'What's going on? Are you all right?'

'It's all in this book that Dick gave me. It's opened my eyes about modern living and modern eating, about the number of ways modern food is making us sick. It's shocking – truly *shocking* – and I can't bear to keep making food for all of you that is so bad for us.'

She let this sink in. On principle, it was certainly hard to argue with.

Anne had the light of recently acquired fervour in her eye. She was sure of her position and not willing to be talked out of it. As they picked at their food, she expounded on the subjects of wellness, naturopathy, macrobiotic eating, superfoods, mindfulness, balance, the removal of negative emotions and the cultivation of inner honesty. She spoke from the heart, and with a desperate joy that she hoped soon to see in their eyes too. For the moment, however, all she saw was suspicion deepening into bewildered dread.

'So what's the upshot of this, old girl?' asked Julian, his voice trembling with an effort to sound cheerful. 'It sounds

*They'd already made a trip to an upmarket pet store
and purchased all-organic dry food that eradicated all
factory-processed feed.*

wonderful and all that – I mean, we're certainly all for it – but what will we . . . have to do?'

And so Anne explained. From now on, the whole lot of them were going to eat only whole food. No processed 'muck', no additives. All organic. Timmy included – there were to be no exceptions. Anne had already made a trip to an upmarket pet store and purchased (at eye-watering expense) all-organic dry food that eradicated all factory-processed feed from his diet. (Which, it turned out, made up one hundred per cent of what he had been eating these last fifteen years.)

'It's part of a process called "clean eating",' said Anne. 'We may not be sick now, but we will be if we continue eating the foods that we're surrounded with. The meat we eat comes from animals that are farmed under absolutely ghastly circumstances, pumped full of steroids and all sorts of terrible things. In all processed foods there are additives, genetic modifications, impure things that we can't know the consequences of.'

'Of which we cannot know the consequences,' said Julian quietly.

'Within a month, we're going to be clean and lean enough to grace the cover of *Vogue*. You mark my words.'

'I agree that this sounds great, and I'm all behind it. But I'm just wondering,' put in George, 'if we should seek further expert advice to back up the – how much have you read, first thirty pages? – of a cookery book.'

'It's not a cookbook, it's a *lifestyle manual*. But I was thinking about this in advance, dear George, and so I've made an appointment for us all tomorrow at a local nutritionist so you can see that I'm right. Soon, we'll all be healthier and happier than ever.'

'Hurray for you, Anne!' said Dick.

'Woof!' said Timmy, wagging his tail.

CHAPTER THREE

A Surprising Health Specialist

In the bathroom, next morning, Anne examined herself in the mirror. She really wasn't sure if the new diet was noticeable *quite* yet, and, weighing herself, she saw no detectable change. She couldn't help feeling a little disappointed – although the diet was only one meal old, she *felt* as though she should be enjoying some of the benefits already. She was certainly feeling saintly.

After a lunch of salmon and quinoa cakes, all four of them, with Timmy in tow, walked down to the high street, where a complementary health therapist had recently set up shop.

'Well, if it's truly complimentary, they won't be expecting a fee!' Julian said. He expected the others to laugh and, when they didn't, he let out a little chuckle to encourage them. But they weren't listening.

The title over the window was *WELLNESS WISDOM*, beneath which was written, in smaller capitals, SPECIALISTS IN BODY AWARENESS, SPIRITUAL CURATION AND NATURAL HOLISTIC REMEDIES. George tied Timmy up outside, while the others debated what the strapline was supposed to mean.

They entered to find themselves in a cross between a doctor's waiting room and a cosmetic boutique. Everything (the walls, the products, the assistant's coat) was a soothing cream colour and there were posters on the walls of beautiful naked women, in full make-up, receiving a variety of treatments and smiling. The complete lack of a picture of a man on any of the clinic's promotional literature made Dick somewhat apprehensive, and Julian suspicious.

They were each offered a cup of nettle tea, which they peered into while Anne explained to the assistant about their booking. Presently, they were shown down a corridor and into the spacious consultation room beyond. Glancing round as they entered, the four flatmates saw a couch, certificates on the walls, posters boasting the health benefits of various regimes, a bookcase showing many colourful spines of health books, and, behind a desk – their cousin, Rupert!

They were all flabbergasted, and made varying noises of astonishment and delight. If Timmy had been allowed in, he would have barked.

'RUPERT!' George yelled. 'What the devil are *you* doing here?'

Cousin Rupert, for his part, took the situation entirely in

his stride. He was a tall, handsome fellow of about forty: immaculately dressed, glossy and imperturbable. He tilted his seat back soundlessly and put his hands behind his head in a pose of carefree ease.

'Within a month, we're going to be clean and lean enough to grace the cover of Vogue. *You mark my words.'*

'Darling cousins,' he drawled. 'Simply helping people, and nothing more. Curing the ailments of the masses, one at a time.'

For Julian, the initial pleasant surprise waned quickly as he recalled the last time he'd heard from Cousin Rupert. 'But I thought you were in . . .' He checked over his shoulder to be sure the assistant had left the room, and lowered his voice. 'Well, in prison. In . . . was it Ecuador?'

'Oh, no, no,' said Rupert, waving a hand. 'I mean, I *was*, but all that business is water under the bridge now. A simple misunderstanding. Please, all of you, sit. Make yourselves comfortable.'

They did so, hesitantly. 'Because they said you were . . . I mean . . . there were some pretty awful accusations.'

'I was in the import–export trade. A humble merchant. How those things came to be on one of my boats is a mystery' – he saw he was struggling to win them over, and his expression flickered from utter innocence to profound sorrow – 'and a matter of great anger and sadness to me. But I have come to peace with those who perpetrated it. I forgive them.'

The four of them took this in for a moment, but could not think of what to say.

Anne could not bear social awkwardness under any circumstances, and felt especially responsible in this situation because she had brought these parties together, so she eagerly moved the conversation on. 'I never knew that you were . . . an expert in . . . all this.'

'All my life,' said Rupert emphatically. 'Despite my other careers, I have always maintained a strong interest in medicine and well-being, always kept up with the latest trends and treatments. During my unfortunate incarceration in South America, I was left alone with my books. After reading so much, I knew I had to set up a practice to pass on what wisdom I had gained. So here I am. Now, enough about me. Tell me what ails *you* . . .'

This, Anne proceeded to do. She explained how her eyes had been opened to the toxic nature of the modern Western diet, how horrified she had been to discover that, by living the lives they were living, they were running themselves down into the ground and making themselves sick. Rupert nodded along wisely with all that she said.

'You mentioned gluten just now,' he said at the end.

'That's right, I'm concerned that it—'

'POISON,' said Rupert. He leant back and yodelled at the ceiling. '*We're poisoning ourselves*, Anne! I think, like many patients, you have riddled your way through to the root of your own problem. You want to get that out of your diet *right now*.'

Anne beamed at this confirmation of her suspicions.

'It is imperative that you start this diet at once,' said Rupert. 'No gluten. No dairy. NO sugar. It is essential for your well-being – physical, mental and spiritual – that you cut these foods out immediately. By the way, may I make a guess? That book you're reading, it's *Perfectly Portia*, right?'

Anne squeaked with delight. 'How did you know?'

'Oh, I live by that book,' he said. 'And Portia's a close personal friend. Silvio Berlusconi introduced us at a party. Wonderful night, wonderful woman. A true guru, and a gymnast to boot. Now, we have some leaflets that will show you what foods to avoid, and how best to do it. Then I want you back here in a fortnight to tell me how you're doing.'

Anne was gushing with her thanks, but Rupert did not seem overly interested. 'Great to see you all,' he said, smiling briefly. 'Maureen, in reception, has the leaflets for you.'

'I say,' said Julian as he got up, his voice thick with uncharacteristic diffidence, 'seeing as you're so near, we really ought to have you over for dinner . . .'

'Terribly busy,' said Rupert, again flashing his fast, emphatic smile. He turned back to his computer screen and began tapping.

Impressed by his abruptness, they all began to drift towards the door. Only George hung back. 'What does "curation"

16

*Weighing herself, she saw no detectable change. Although the diet was only one meal old, she **felt** as though she should be enjoying some of the benefits already.*

mean?' she asked. 'In the tag line for your business.'

'Fancy word for curing. The business of making better,' said Rupert without looking up from his screen.

'I don't think it does,' said George.

Rupert frowned, typed a few words and hit enter. Then he read for a moment and looked off to his left. 'In which case,' he said, 'it means that we offer a multifaceted approach to medicine, taking from many cultures and disciplines. And it is our wide knowledge of those that are curated for our patients. Making for a truly *holistic* approach.'

All four of the flatmates turned again to leave, nodding thoughtfully.

Back at reception, they were handed the requisite leaflets from the somewhat put-upon Maureen, along with an invoice.

'Four *hundred* pounds?' asked Julian, opening it before Anne could get her hands on it.

'For the consultation,' said Maureen.

'But we were only in there ten minutes. Let me go back and ask him – this is an outrage – I'm his cousin!' said Julian.

'He told me to apply "mates' rates",' said Maureen flatly. 'Usually, for group consultation, it would be six hundred.'

Anne goggled and George swore beneath her breath as Julian handed over his Barclaycard with a face like stone.

'And I suppose that's before VAT,' he added bitterly.

When they stood outside again, they quietly thanked Julian for paying for the consultation, and each offered somewhat feeble promises to pay him back for their share soon. He nodded stiffly and maintained a distant stare.

'Still,' said Anne brightly. 'This is an *adventure*, isn't it?

Like we used to have! And we're doing it together, aren't we?'

'I guess we are,' said George, trying to untie an eager Timmy despite his frantic efforts to lick her face.

'Of *course* we are,' said Dick. 'It's a new kind of adventure, and we have only you to thank, Anne!'

'Woof!' said Timmy, with approval.

Anne beamed. The new cleaner, fitter, happier Anne was just around the corner . . . She couldn't wait to get started!

CHAPTER FOUR

The New Regime

When they got home that evening, Anne went through the fridge, freezer and kitchen cupboards, checking every packet to weed out what she described as 'the foods of shame'. It was only after she had finished, three hours later, that she realized she should have just removed all their food. The only items that had survived under the new regime were some tins of tuna, half a packet of currants, and a pot of black olives in brine covered with a mouldy scum.

It made for an enormous pile on the kitchen table, which Anne proceeded to bag up and take down to the bins. Once again, she did this solo, as George claimed to have a judo lesson, Dick had declared himself 'too weak to walk', having been denied his morning bacon sandwich, and Julian said the rounding-up process of suspicious foods was too disturbingly 'Orwellian' and he would have no part in it. (He never liked to miss an opportunity to turn a conversation towards his degree in English Literature from Oxford University.)

Anne decided to learn from the lessons of her reading, and

balance herself. She went to her room and shut the door, drew the curtains and took off her shoes. She sat in the middle of the floor and crossed her legs, then laid her wrists on her knees and shut her eyes. She took deep breaths.

Her breathing slowed and her breaths grew deeper. As the one leading this change in lifestyle, she must set an example.

'What on earth is this?' interrupted Julian.
'It's cauliflower rice,' said Anne.
'So is it rice? Or cauliflower? I'm confused.'

She drew her senses inwards, and sought connection and acceptance.

She breathed. She listened to her own breath.

Then, as she relaxed, her thoughts moving as slowly and ponderously as an elephant trying not to tread on snails, she attempted to 'achieve presence'. She did this by perceiving herself and the fact that she was in this room, being a person. Slowly she expanded her consciousness beyond the room, and became aware of a rhythmic thumping noise coming from the kitchen.

She breathed. Gradually she recognized the thumping sound as that of Dick's trainers in the washer-dryer. With calm objective peacefulness, Anne realized she was about to get up, and go and take those trainers out of the washer-dryer, and jolly well give Dick a good yelling at.

CHAPTER FIVE

Planning Ahead

'It says here,' Anne stated at that evening's meal, 'that we should plan for—'

'What on earth's this?' interrupted Julian, forking over the strange pale mass on his plate.

'It's cauliflower rice,' said Anne.

'So is it rice? Or cauliflower? I'm confused,' Julian said, peering down at it with wondering curiosity. 'Courgette spaghetti, cauliflower rice,' he mused. 'What's next?'

'I'll go first!' said Dick, always eager to make a game of something. He frowned with concentration. 'Vegetable made into a carbohydrate,' he muttered, looking about the room. 'How about, er . . . carrot . . . potato?'

'Don't be stupid, Dick,' said George pleasantly. 'Julian, it's a rice substitute made from blended cauliflower. Anne, please go on.'

'It says here,' Anne repeated doggedly, 'that, if we want to succeed on the diet, we should be honest about when we're likely to fall down on it. And plan ahead, so that we don't.

Very good idea, I think. So,' she said, putting the book down, 'what do we think are our danger zones? And let's plan to avoid them.'

'This Friday,' said Julian. 'It's the birthday party for Archie from Monday five-a-side. That will get messy.'

'Do you have to go?'

'Absolutely,' said Dick, nodding vehemently. 'The boys would be terribly upset if we weren't there.'

'Okay, well, we can think our way around this,' said Anne. 'The boys will be drinking beer?'

'Let me think,' said Julian. 'Dick, will the boys be drinking beer?'

The thing Dick most hated in the world, above protracted foreign wars and virulent outbreaks of plague, was the sight of Julian using high-handed sarcasm on Anne. He hurried to explain the reality of the situation to her.

'They will *all* drink a *lot* of beer,' he said. 'And rum, whisky, vodka, and cocktails, maybe, and shooters, and— Frankly, it would be quicker to list the things that they won't be drinking.'

'Well, you could drink cranberry juice?' said Anne. 'Or, I read a blog full of tips about how to survive nights out without drinking, and someone suggested dipping the rim of a glass in gin and filling it up with tonic water. Apparently, you'd never know it wasn't the real thing! Really, we should be avoiding alcohol, if possible.'

Dick, the diplomat, chewed his lip, looking for a solution. On the one hand, Anne was the dearest thing to him in the world. And, on the other, he had seen the boys out together before. For his own birthday, in fact – and that had certainly been an adventure, finding his way back from Doncaster railway station the next morning, without a wallet or trousers. One he did not relish repeating.

'Define "if possible",' put in Julian. 'Let's look closely at this "if possible" and what it covers. You mean it would be acceptable for religious reasons? And, say, in a hostage situation?' Julian had always rather fancied himself as a barrister. If Anne took this particular piece of bait, he was vaguely hoping that the definition of either 'hostage scenario' or 'religious observance' might be stretched to include peer pressure at a birthday party.

Anne smiled pleasurelessly at him. She wanted to be reasonable. 'I think you should have a nice drink with your friends,' she said. 'But just avoid having too much, because then you will want greasy food and other unhealthy drinks, and we will be back to square one.'

'Message received and understood,' said Julian, giving a warning nod to Dick to stop him asking for any more detailed

After a lunch of salmon and quinoa cakes, they walked down to the high street where a complementary health therapist had recently set up shop.

delineation of their specific drinking allowance, in case it was more restrictive.

'George,' said Anne. 'What are your temptations?'

'Well, I work with tech nerds who eat sandwiches and croissants and cakes all day,' she said. Anne opened her mouth to answer but George went on. 'And crisps and sweets, and pizza and kebabs. And pasties. Ice creams. Sweet drinks. Chocolate. It's a wonder any of them are alive,' she said.

'Hmm,' said Anne. 'Then I'll make you a nice alfalfa salad to take to work each day, and some celery to snack on.'

George thought about this for a moment. 'Why are we on this diet again?' she asked.

'To be healthier, happier, fuller, *better* people. It's an adventure!' Anne said with a brilliant smile. 'And now me. I'm concerned that, after hot yoga on Wednesdays, I often go to the café with Petronella and Olivia and we usually have a slice of what can feel like well-earned cake. But I will steel myself and just have a fruit tea. I'm so happy we're doing this! Aren't you all?'

'Woof!' said Timmy, more out of habit than enthusiasm. He lowered his head and took a mouthful of the dry food in his bowl, chewing it slowly. In fact, he remained as sceptical as the rest of them.

The others merely looked thoughtful, and avoided each other's eye.

CHAPTER SIX

The First Week

And so the five housemates entered into their new, enriched life. Breakfast, being the most important meal of the day, was something that, for the first few days, Anne put an extra special effort into making pleasurable for them all. They enjoyed breakfasts of scrambled eggs, smoked salmon, organic bacon and sausages, grilled halloumi, blueberries and other fresh fruits. And, with these treats, Anne tutored them to replace their morning tea and coffee with hot water and lemon.

Each evening, when they came home from work and took Timmy for a walk round the park, Anne would catch up with the others to see how their day had been, and, more importantly, how the diet was going.

She found this a little hard going at first, because, in contrast to her bouncy enthusiasm, they were all feeling somewhat lethargic. Their usual energy levels seemed, for now, at least, to be drastically depleted by the change in diet. George and Julian reported problems sleeping, owing to hunger, and Dick said nothing at all, but threw sticks for Timmy (harder and further than usual, because he pictured them as the celery sticks he was now obliged to eat instead of biscuits), partly to try to keep himself awake. Anne assured them that their sleep, when it had normalized, would be much improved. And it didn't stop there – they would have improved bowels, clearer skin, fewer headaches . . .

'But, dear girl, we didn't have any of those problems in the first place,' said Julian.

'Oh, darling Ju, don't you see? All these things will improve so much, you'll suddenly realize how unhealthy your previous lifestyle was.'

'Please don't call him "Ju", Anne,' said George. 'People might be listening. We've been over this. He's Julian, or Jules at a push. You just can't go around calling someone "Ju" anymore.'

'Oh, look,' said Anne. 'Timmy's done his business. George, have you got a b—? Oh, my!'

This routine was second nature to George, so she already had the requisite bag in hand. As the others recoiled, she stared down at the offending mess with the look of a grizzled detective standing over the victim of some fresh mutilation.

'This new diet is certainly having an effect on *his* gut,' said Anne.

'No way *that's* gonna go in a bag,' said George, glancing

One by one, they retired to bed with achingly empty stomachs.

left and right. 'You'd need a hoover. Nothing to see here, people. Nothing to see. Let's all be on our way. We haven't seen anything . . . You feeling okay, Timmy? Do I need to be worried? Because this looks like diseased alien snot.'

'Woof,' Timmy assured her, trotting ahead with his tail between his legs.

*

As the days went on, Anne found it harder to maintain the front of unblinking positivity that she liked to project, and that she felt was her pleasurable lot in life. The fact was, planning ahead to withstand them didn't make the temptations of modern city living drastically less tempting.

In her office, Anne sat opposite a couple who (it was common knowledge, despite the fact that they thought they were keeping it secret) were having an affair. Each morning, one of them brought in Danish pastries for them both, which they ate with their coffee at about 11 a.m. For some reason, knowing in advance about this love-in carb-fest seemed to make it worse for Anne. She had no interest in their reprehensible extramural activities, but she found something immoral and lascivious about the way they ate these sweetmeats, right there in front of her, savouring every bite and laughing rather too loudly at each other's jokes. Each morning, at that time, Anne ate half a packet of blueberries, and tried to avert her gaze.

At lunchtime, everyone in Anne's office went to the subsidized canteen, where there were several main courses available, all with different names, but all consisting of slop served from stainless-steel tanks, invariably in a dense, flour-thickened sauce. The thing about this food was that, although it was certainly unpleasant, it was also warm, filling, cheap, and convenient. Therefore, most employees tended to eat it, slowly and without pleasure, while complaining about its lack of flavour.

After the first day, Anne realized that she didn't even want to sit in the canteen and watch this, so instead she took her lunch outside, finding a bench in the nearby park. Here, however, she was soon discovered by Mr Temple, the company's health-and-safety man, a short, intense fellow who wore dark glasses at all times. Delighted to find someone else who enjoyed exploring the outdoors, he sat next to her each lunchtime and regaled her with stories of his experiences with the Territorial Army, performing invasion drills with his young sons in the New Forest. Anne never really answered back or told stories of her own, but it didn't seem to matter. Even Anne, who would have liked to read her Georgette Heyer paperback in peace, had to admit this was not entirely ideal.

The diet was certainly presenting its challenges. And what was worse, despite being eight or ten pious meals into it, she still did not notice a difference in the mirror. Nor one on the bathroom scales that was dramatic enough to put down to anything other than standard fluctuation. It didn't seem fair.

On the third evening, the housemates were eating steamed spiralized sweet potato with an organic pesto made from basil, oregano, kale, nettle leaves and macadamia nuts. As usual,

THE FIRST WEEK

Timmy hunted round the table, panting, waiting for a sympathetic diner to give him some cast-off scraps. He never did this in vain, because they all loved him so much and couldn't bear the idea of him being tantalized by the smell of their superior food. Someone would always give him a bite or two off their plate.

Today, however, he had hit the jackpot. At each chair he nosed around, he found handfuls of spiralized new potato being dangled beneath the table and then dropped on the floor for him. He inspected each pile of food with his nose, and then moved on hopefully to the next. At last, he returned to his basket and curled up there with his head resting on the rim, nose jutting over the heap of organic, additive-free 'all-in-one' dry food that Anne had poured out for him, and he had not touched. The housemates each, in turn, gave his bowl an appraising, hungry glance.

Looking up at his beloved masters, he thought of sausages. He didn't bark.

After dinner, a tense silence fell in the room, with no one really paying attention to the tasteful new John le Carré adaptation on TV. This meant they all watched Timmy as he rose from Anne's lap, walked over to the television and, as the camera lingered upon a fantastically rich-looking dessert, licked the screen, making a long, discordant, window-cleaning squeak, and leaving a glistening neon smear of saliva across the picture, the length of a child's arm.

The spell was broken. Julian said that, as far as he knew, there had been serious food shortages in the Eastern bloc at the time this drama was set, and he wasn't going to sit around watching such inaccurate tosh. He got up and went to bed, with everyone else shortly following suit. Anne finally switched the telly off and polished the screen with a tissue; Timmy watched, panting happily as he waited for the pictures of food to come on again, so he could have another lick.

CHAPTER SEVEN

Time for a Change

If there was one thing that happy, cheerful, positive Anne prided herself on, it was gauging the mood of the house. And, despite the fact that she knew their diet would make them healthier and happier in the long run, she also knew that it was being stuck in their ordinary routines that was making it difficult to get used to the new regime.

George admitted straight-up she'd eaten a slice of chocolate cake at a function for a departing work colleague. (In fact, she commented on the deliciousness of the crème-fraiche icing.) Julian and Dick had both come into the kitchen looking decidedly sorry for themselves after their Friday-night birthday do, and an examination of the kitchen bin provided incriminating evidence of the consumption of late-night kebabs. Anne herself had snapped and eaten half a biscuit on Thursday afternoon.

They needed a change: a sudden, quick and complete change. It would be easy to startle themselves out of their bad habits if they were in a new environment.

The new cleaner, fitter, happier Anne was just around the corner. She couldn't wait to get started!

Therefore, the next Tuesday evening, she presented them with a plan. They were to have an impromptu holiday.

'Kirrin Island!' yelled Dick. 'What a wonderful idea!'

George and Julian, as Anne had expected, were a tad more sceptical.

'But we can pursue a diet up here in the city as well as anywhere else,' George said.

'And I've got commitments,' protested Julian. 'There's football, and . . . and . . .'

'Now, you know I don't want to be a scold,' said Anne, 'but we all know the temptations being put in our way are too much. They're intolerable! All around us, we see people eating whatever they like, whenever they like, and of course this makes us want to do the same. We'll never really fulfil the dream of being natural and whole and pure while we're here. Not unless we've already got a few weeks' success under our belt.'

'Oh, Anne,' said Julian, chuckling. 'One little mistake is to be expected. We're made of sterner stuff than you think. Give us one more chance and we'll prove you wrong.'

Anne looked sad. 'I'm sorry you're making me do this,' she said softly, 'but you have allowed me to clean your rooms for the last year, and so it was with sorrow that I came across these items.' One after the other, she placed on the table an empty

Ginsters pasty wrapper, an empty packet of Jelly Babies, and a Big Mac carton.

'I won't say which was found where,' she said quietly, 'only that you know what you've done.'

One by one, she met their eyes, and each of them looked away. Timmy gazed at them with no less accusation, as he was able to smell the delicious foods that had been consumed within these walls – and not by him.

'This is an adventure,' Anne said. 'If all of us aren't going on it, none of us is.'

Julian blustered for a moment, but quickly gave up.

'Fine. You're right. It's no good doing this here. Let's go to Dorset.'

CHAPTER EIGHT

The Journey, Not the Destination

None of them had taken a holiday all year, and so each was able to bargain some leave at short notice. Friday evening saw them gathered at Waterloo station, printing off their advance tickets at the self-service machine, while Timmy jumped around and attempted to make friends with all the interesting-smelling people that were passing by.

'Come on,' said Anne, 'our tickets are specific to this train; we can't miss it.'

'We KNOW that, Anne, thank you,' said Julian, still trying to read the booking code off the screen of his phone with considerable frustration. 'We all knew it before we got here, and you have told us again five times since. We are hideously early. We cannot catch the train *more* than we are already going to catch it.' As the ticket machine failed for the third time to recognize the code he entered, Julian straightened his back and yodelled at the glass roof high above, scattering a group of gossiping pigeons. Anne announced she was going to go and find somewhere that would serve her a turmeric latte.

'Here, give it to me,' said Dick, grabbing his brother's phone.

'Why don't we just have *tickets*, and people who sell you tickets, and station masters, and station porters, and politeness, rather than all this dehumanizing rigmarole?' Julian asked the air above his head.

'And steam trains, and all good old-fashioned things?' asked George.

'Well, yes!'

'What can I say?' George replied. 'It's gone, buddy.'

'I just don't *like* the modern world,' huffed Julian.

'Ah, that's just the lentil salad talking,' said George cheerfully.

'Here's your ticket,' Dick said, handing it over to Julian. 'Come on. Platform eleven.'

'We have to catch this train,' said Anne, returning with cup in hand. 'This *particular* one.'

'We KNOW that!'

They were in plenty of time as they arrived at their coach, loaded their bags in the appropriate storage spaces, and took their seats. Usually they would be rushing, owing to the various gluten-, dairy-, caffeine- and alcohol-rich treats that a railway terminus offers. Now, however, all these were off-limits, and so they had nothing to do but wait for others to board the

'We're going to eat no wheat, no dairy, no sugar,'
explained George.
'I'm so pleased,' said Aunt Fanny. 'Shall I make you
some nice peanut butter sandwiches for your picnic?'

train as Anne pleasantly and repeatedly explained to various passengers that they had indeed booked these exact seats.

'Oh, I say, I forgot that I've brought you a treat,' said Anne, producing a Tupperware container. By this point, the others were somewhat jaundiced towards anything Anne described as a 'treat'. They reacted to the objects that were now offered to them – which looked rather like small falafels – with polite indifference, like an elderly aunt shown a painting by a toddler to whom she is not related.

'Power balls,' Anne said.

Dick had already picked one of these things up out of pure politeness. Hearing its name, he dropped it in his lap.

'It sounds like a football show on a cheap cable channel,' said Julian. 'Presented by glamour models.'

'It sounds like a Spanish business book from the 1980s,' said Dick.

'It sounds like a remake of *House of Cards*, set in the world of Jane Austen,' said George, joining in.

'It doesn't matter what the name sounds like,' said Anne testily. 'Yes, we *have* booked these seats, *thank* you. Yes, these *are* our seats, seeing as you ask. It doesn't matter,' she continued at a quieter volume, 'what the name reminds you of.'

'Of what the name reminds you,' muttered Julian, looking out of the window.

'It sounds like a late-nineties sitcom starring Martin Clunes,' said Dick. 'About a sports agent called Power, who's had a vasectomy.'

'I think of it,' said George, 'as the name of an imported energy drink that has been banned in fourteen Asian countries.'

'Yes,' said Julian. '"Look at that poor bloke; he really looks like he's been hitting the vodka Power Balls." That sort of thing.'

The train began its gentle glide out of the station.

'Well, I'm glad you're able to amuse yourselves,' said Anne. 'But these power balls are truffles made of ground nuts, dates, coconut oil, and a dusting of cacao.'

They each took one and nibbled it, in order to be polite. They had no idea how they would ordinarily feel about this food. But, in their present state, it was certainly a pleasant surprise. A veritable treat, in fact.

The four contented themselves with the view of a steadily retreating south London as the train swished acceleratingly towards the south coast. The journey passed pleasantly. By the time the carriage was illuminated by sunlight reflecting off the Solent, the box of power balls was empty. The only slight unpleasantness was when Julian pointed out to someone talking on his phone that this was the quiet carriage, a situation quickly soothed by George explaining to Julian that he was being considerably louder and more disruptive than the man on his phone.

The wide, pleasant countryside of Dorset opened up around

them, bathed in a gentle blue evening sunshine, and, as the train glided through it, Timmy snoozed under George's seat and the rest of them sighed with the relief of returning once more to a home away from home. Anne was right – this whole clean-eating thing must be easier when surrounded by lush countryside and fresh air. They were determined to turn over a new spinach leaf – this could really be the start of something!

CHAPTER NINE

A Surprise About Kirrin Island

They were met at the station by Uncle Quentin. Despite the fact that they were no longer children, but qualified urban professionals, Uncle Quentin had not softened his stance towards them. He had always been somewhat narrowly focused, and with age this had turned into something bordering on taciturn crankiness. All young visitors, to him, were hazards to the sanctity of his work, his peace, and his state of mind. But, by this stage, they were all used to his ways and didn't mind a bit.

'Hullo, Daddy,' said George, hopping in the front seat and pecking him on the cheek.

'Yes,' he said. He was firmly gripping the steering wheel and looking out of the windscreen. The others threw their luggage in the boot, piled into the back seat, and he immediately pulled out of the car park at high speed, narrowly avoiding a lady with a pram.

'How are you, Uncle?' asked Dick cheerfully.

'Yes,' Quentin said again.

'He's quite distracted,' said George. 'As usual, he's probably in the middle of one of his experiments. Aren't you, Daddy?' said George.

'Yes,' said Quentin, putting his arm out of the window to signal for a turn.

'I say, Uncle,' said Dick, 'isn't it interesting that they've just discovered that albatrosses live to the age of a million, which means that, from now on, chairs are going to be able to vote in Norway?'

'Yes,' said Quentin grimly.

'I love it when you do that,' whispered Anne to Dick.

'I say, Uncle,' said Julian, 'isn't it funny that—'

'Oh, shut up, you lot,' said George.

'Yes,' agreed Uncle Quentin.

They all looked out of the windows as the sunny countryside span by.

Once they were out of town and into the countryside, Uncle Quentin began to relax a little. His shoulders unhunched at least a fraction and he began to breathe regularly. They knew, now, they could engage him in what was as close to normal conversation as you could ever get with him – once home, he would disappear into the laboratory and return only for meals.

'I say, Uncle Quentin,' said Julian, 'I've not seen this car before. Is it new?'

'It's called "courgetti". That's spaghetti made from courgette. It tastes just like the real thing – you won't notice the difference.'

'Glad you asked, young tyke,' said Quentin. 'This is my latest experiment. Carbon-free fuel's the way to go now, right? Well, you see, this thing runs on peanuts.'

'Frightfully cheap to run, is it?'

'No; it literally runs on peanut oil. And whole peanuts, if you pour them in the crusher at the back. That's that awful noise you can hear. And also why I was so nervous in town. It's totally illegal.'

'I imagine there are all sorts of tests that a new engine has to go through before it's roadworthy,' said George.

'Partly that. But also it's *incredibly* dangerous. Could blow up at any minute. Has anyone got a cigarette?'

They all yelled that they hadn't.

'Woof!' said Timmy disapprovingly.

'Hmm, that's a shame. Only chance I get, these days, is on these little jaunts away from the house.'

'Can we get out and walk?' asked Anne from the back.

'Certainly not,' said Quentin, suddenly speeding up. 'I'm not explaining to my wife that I left you out here, in the middle of nowhere. She'd kill me.' The little peanut car mounted a hill, offering a distant view of Kirrin Island, and Quentin's expression cleared, just as all the others in the car were looking more worried than ever. 'So, what will you be up to while you're here, then?'

'It's a health break, more than anything,' said George. 'We'll go to the island, of course.'

'Which island?' asked Quentin.

George regarded him oddly. 'What do you mean, which island? Kirrin Island. The one I own.' She tried to overcome her temper at her father's obtuseness, and failed. 'Why would you *pretend not to know* that's what I mean?' she asked.

'There's no going to the island,' Quentin said, his eyes on the road ahead.

In a purely scientific way, he might have been expected to know this remark would upset his daughter. But the dominant scientist section of his brain rarely allowed information to filter through to the smaller, fathering part. Therefore, when George gave a loud protesting shout, he swerved across the road, only narrowly missing an oncoming truck. Everyone in the back seats shouted unanimously.

'Woof!' said Timmy, even more disapprovingly than ever. 'Woof, woof!'

'You mean, no one's allowed to go to the island except me, right? Because it's *mine*?'

'N—'

'And *I* decide who does and doesn't go there?' continued George.

'Not exactly,' said Quentin.

49

'Because I *own* it?'

'There was a visit from DEFRA,' said Uncle Quentin. 'I thought your mother told you. It turns out there is an endangered species of vole that lives on Kirrin Island, not found anywhere else on the south coast. It's been designated a Special Area of Conservation. No humans allowed. Which makes it rather exclusive, don't you think?'

Those in the back seat watched George with apprehension. They were driving, at this moment, down a narrow coast road that offered stunning views, but no second chances to the imprecise driver.

After a long pause, George asked, 'Does that mean no one's allowed to go there?'

'No one at all,' said Uncle Quentin cheerfully.

George fell naturally, it must be said, upon the left side of the political spectrum. She had enjoyed her time at university in Brighton, which she considered the spiritual home of her adulthood. But this revelation about Kirrin Island caught her off guard, and she found herself muttering the phrase 'political correctness gone mad' under her breath. At length, however, she said aloud, in a more cheerful voice, 'Well, if there are vulnerable little voles crawling about on the island, I bet there's one dog I know who couldn't help but to chase them. Isn't that right, Timmy?'

'Woof!' said Timmy.

Everyone breathed a sigh of relief.

'So, if their lives must be spared, then I suppose we must keep away from the place.'

'So what *will* we do with our holiday, then?' asked Dick.

'Get some nice fresh air, stay away from the house, and keep out of my way?' Quentin suggested, swerving on to the causeway that led to the house with such violence he made everyone in the car bounce a foot into the air.

'Woof!' said Timmy, with excitement.

The chassis reconnected with the ground with a mighty crash. Luckily, the car did not explode.

Aunt Fanny was delighted to see them all, and showed them to their old rooms (and basket).

'Your two beds are getting a tad small for you now,' she said to Anne and Dick, 'but it's your own fault for keeping growing!' They both assured her with such honest fervency of their nostalgia for the little beds they had slept in as children that she could not feel guilty for offering them again.

'Now, I've made you a nice tea,' said Aunt Fanny, when everyone was assembled. She gestured to the table, which was covered with a selection of tarts, quiches, buns and pastries – surely the product of several days' concerted labour.

'I'll make you a nice alfalfa salad to take to work
each day,' said Anne.
George thought about this for a moment.
'Why are we on this diet again?' she asked.

George looked wary, however.

'The second I heard you were coming,' Fanny said, 'I went into overdrive. It's such a treat to have you all here at once. Why, it's been years.'

She had already cut four slices from a Victoria sponge with a cream-and-fruit centre, which she was handing out on plates. George held her hand up, and Fanny hesitated. Julian, in reaching out for the cake and nearly touching it, saw this, and also hesitated. For a moment, they made a tableau.

'Mummy, this is all wonderful. But you did get my email, I hope?' asked George. 'About our dietary restrictions?'

'Well, no,' said Aunt Fanny. 'I haven't checked my email since Easter. It's been so busy round here!'

George turned to look at the other items on the table that had been assembled for their tea. She put her hand down and stroked Timmy's neck in such a gentle, mournful fashion that he let out a keening sound.

'Mummy,' George said, 'I'm afraid I've got some bad news . . .'

CHAPTER TEN

'Free-From' Everything at Kirrin Cottage

It turned out that bad news was something that could be very difficult indeed to communicate to the inhabitants of Kirrin Cottage. The first reason for this was that one of Uncle Quentin's experiments had knocked out the cottage's broadband and they hadn't managed to get it up and running again for the past six months, rendering the family PC largely useless.

Emails were something Fanny now could only access when she caught the bus into town to have tea with her sister-in-law (cousin Rupert's mother, a fearful snob), who visited fortnightly from Dorchester. But that also relied on the library still being open after they'd talked for a few hours, and (if she did have enough time) her being in the right mood to remember, which usually depended on whether they'd quarrelled. Which, in summation, meant it was a rare event. So George's lengthy email explaining all their dietary requirements had gone entirely unheeded.

George, having only ever received seven emails from her parents, had been well aware this might happen, however.

Which was why she had texted the gist of these dietary requirements to her mother as a back-up communication.

'Oh, yes, I remember; that was last Thursday. Well, I was going to read it, but just as I picked up my phone, your cousin Rupert called with the news about his baby. Isn't it wonderful? A girl. Have a sausage roll, Dick.'

Standing next to a table creaking with food they wanted but could not have, her guests regarded Fanny's soon-to-be-extinguished innocence with terrible sorrow.

'This new diet is certainly having an effect on his gut,' said Anne.

That was when George discovered that it was difficult to pass on the gist of bad news to the inhabitants of Kirrin Cottage, even by telling them face to face. She tried her best, and yet, despite her finest attempt, Fanny did not seem to understand.

'It's just so nice to *have* you here,' she said. 'Everyone will be so happy. It's been such a long time . . .'

They could not bear to respond to Aunt Fanny's enthusiasm with anything other than the gratitude it deserved, and so they all gave her a big hug and said how nice it was to be there. Then they all protested they were so stuffed, they couldn't manage a thing, and one by one they retired to bed with achingly empty stomachs.

First thing the next morning, they found themselves all congregating back in the kitchen, where Aunt Fanny was putting the last touches on a pie.

'What's in there, dearest aunt in the whole world?' asked Dick.

'Ham,' said Aunt Fanny distractedly.

'Yum!' said Dick.

'Chicken, leek and herbs,' Aunt Fanny continued.

Everyone oohed and aahed.

'Cream,' she went on, 'sherry, morels and some leftover rabbit.'

'Woof!' said Timmy, in response to the word 'rabbit'.

This, then, was to be their evening meal.

It now fell to George, once and for all, to get through to Aunt Fanny forcefully what she had so far tried and failed to communicate so many times. At the end, Aunt Fanny was still smiling, and saying she thought it was a nice idea.

'But we can't eat this food,' said George. 'This delicious pie – which is, may I point out to everyone else, my *favourite* pie – we can't have any of it. Or that tart, or those buns or sausage rolls you've stacked back in the pantry.'

'Maybe just have a little bit,' Fanny said.

'We can't. That's the whole point of being on a gluten-free diet,' said George.

'Well,' Fanny said, unperturbed, 'we'll see if anyone wants some later.'

'Oh, we'll *want* some,' said George, 'because it's delicious. But we're not allowed to eat it, and therefore we won't. Because, for better or worse, we're all doing this together. We've come on this visit to be healthy and happy, and we're going to eat no wheat, no dairy, no sugar, nothing processed, no salted foods. And we're going to go out and get some fresh air right damn now!'

'I'm so pleased,' said Aunt Fanny. 'Shall I make you some nice peanut-butter sandwiches to take with you?'

CHAPTER ELEVEN

Getting to Know Dorset Again

Anne, Dick and Julian had excused themselves early into George's conversation with Aunt Fanny, rather than witness the rest of the exchange. In fact, having all walked off in separate directions to try and get out of earshot of George's accusations that Aunt Fanny 'wasn't listening, like bloody always', they ended up bumping into each other by the cliff edge behind the house, where they looked down at the surf breaking against the rocks and felt the wind whistling in over the channel – neither of which was able to render George's voice entirely inaudible.

This had always been such a special and happy place for them to visit, and Anne, Dick and Julian took no pleasure in seeing Aunt Fanny try to come to grips with the modern and alien idea that many of the foods she had eaten at every meal in her long, healthy life had now been suddenly deigned poisonous by the younger generation. Eventually, the squall seemed to blow itself out – Aunt Fanny having finally, they assumed, got her head around the idea of their diet – and George joined them at the cliff edge.

And so, to dispel the memory of all these delicious but forbidden foods, they set out for a long walk across the cliffs.

They all trudged merrily ahead all morning, and continued to walk as the afternoon waned and the evening came on. They tumbled down and then they scrambled up the steep slopes, they tramped past cows grazing near the edge, inhaled the intoxicating mixture of flowers and sea and pasture. They walked and climbed for hours and hours, stopping for a lunch of one of Anne's delicious bean salads, before pressing on for a further five or six hours, revelling in the stunning views from every direction, until they were exhausted.

'Can't we stop now?' asked Dick, as they were halfway across one clifftop. The scenery's beauty had not diminished, but the sun was starting to redden and it was time to think about getting home.

'Just take a deep breath and think for a moment about what it means to be,' said Anne. 'What it means to be you, what it means to be here. What it means to be breathing, and thinking.'

'What it means to be near a pub,' said George, pointing at a building in the distance.

'Brillo!' yelled Julian. 'Last one there buys the first round!'

Anne stood on the clifftop alone for a while, breathing deeply and observing her own thoughts, until she felt acceptance and connection, and peace. And thirst.

They were determined to turn over a new spinach leaf.

In a few minutes, she had caught up with the others and they were all ducking under the low roof timbers as they made their way into the pub, debating whether to go and sit outside on the sections of wood log that served instead of stools, or stay inside by the cosy fireplace. It had been a hot day, but was rapidly cooling, and they chose the latter.

As they squeezed along corridors seemingly made for hobbits, there was a vibrant happiness and sense of accomplishment among the group, a ruddy, healthy blush that the Dorset sun had lain upon their complexions, not even diminished when Anne quietly pointed out that ale was not, even after such a virtuous and strenuous hike, part of their diet. They collapsed, giggling, on to wooden benches in the dark and brooding parlour, sending Dick and Julian for drinks.

'Oh, and Ju, see if they have any olives?' called Anne.

'*Julian*,' said George, on the bench next to her. 'Julian, Julian, Julian!'

Owing to the fact that the bar, once you reached it, was not a bar at all but a waist-height hatch over which drinks were handed with a conspiratorial air, Dick, who had thought he was lounging against the wall waiting for his turn, was suddenly surprised to discover himself at the front of the queue.

'Oh! Er, hullo! May I have four pints of soda water with lime, please, and a bowl of water for the dog?' he said.

The landlord, a rather burly fellow who had been chatting animatedly to people further up the queue, licked his teeth and stared at him.

'You serve soda water, surely?' asked Dick. 'It's like ordin-ary water, but fizzy.'

Julian, standing behind Dick, winced. He knew that, from Dick's simple and happy outlook on life, such a remark was meant as an honest explanation. But he also knew it came across as an insult, made only worse by the wide-eyed look that accompanied it.

The landlord fixed Dick with a lengthy, suspicious stare as he began slowly to assemble the requested drinks. Julian noticed that all conversation around them had quietened off a bit. Dick was going rather red. 'Here, gimme those,' muttered Julian, reaching for the first two glasses.

'What snacks do you have?' asked Dick.

The landlord explained gruffly that they served home-made pasties accompanied by mustard, as well as pork scratchings and packets of dry roasted peanuts. A famished Anne chose this moment to join them at the bar, saying she'd often heard of pork scratchings, but had never known what they were. Julian muttered an explanation into her ear and she gagged. But the gorgon hunger could not be so easily assuaged.

'Do you have protein balls?' she asked the landlord.

'Do I have what?' he said.

'Anne,' whispered Julian into her ear, 'that's a perfectly ridiculous question. Go and sit down; you'll get us lynched.'

Dick thanked the landlord, said he wasn't interested in food, after all, and paid for the drinks. As the landlord dipped the change into Dick's hand, his gimlet eye passed over the group.

'You lot think you're funny?' he asked.

'I beg your pardon?'

'I said, do you lot think you're funny?' the landlord repeated, without letting go of Dick's hand.

'Funny in what way, do you mean?' asked Dick.

'Come and sit down, please, Dick – quickly!' called Julian.

The landlord let Dick's hand go and watched him as he walked away. Thereafter, he kept a close eye on the group, while they nervously sipped their soda waters. Anne and George were comparing photographs they had taken on their phones.

'It's not quite as welcoming round here as I remember,' said Julian. 'I don't suppose I've ever been in a pub in Dorset before. Everyone seems to be looking at us rather suspiciously.' He indicated a table of drinkers on the other side of the room, who were muttering and staring.

'What's *happened* to Dorset?' asked George gloomily. 'Everyone's changed.'

'I don't think anyone's ever asked that landlord for soda water before,' said Dick. 'That seemed to be the main trouble. He looked disgusted by the idea of people drinking it, as though it was a drink for animals.'

George held her glass up to the light, feeling in tune with the landlord on that score.

'Perhaps, because we've never been to this particular

pub before, they think we're outsiders. Maybe, around here, they don't like or trust outsiders, and shun them?' Anne suggested nervously. As she finished speaking, she followed the looks of her companions over her shoulder, and found herself face to face with a table of Japanese tourists drinking pints of local ale and giving them glances just as dirty as everyone else.

They all sipped their soda waters for a few minutes, but the conversation which would normally have sprung up after such an enjoyably long hike failed to materialize. They found themselves thinking about food: where their next satisfying meal was going to come from, when it might occur, how they could wait until then. They all thought about how much weight they must have lost already – it had been over a week now, after all – and wondered if they had earned something like a burger and chips. Or one of those delicious-smelling local pasties being devoured by the Japanese tourists . . .

Into such thoughts did they drift as their energy levels subsided, and they lapsed into glum silence. The smells from the next table wafted over them.

'I thought the Japanese didn't eat pastry,' said Julian bitterly.

'Maybe we should leave,' said George. She was tired, so tired. She did not feel as though she had eaten a proper meal in months, and now all she wanted was to be back in her bed,

Anne sipped from her own cup. It really did make you feel alive to drink it – she could almost feel the weight melting off with each sip.

her own childhood bed. She got up to ask the landlord for the number of a local taxi firm.

'Doesn't work,' shrugged the landlord, gesturing at the payphone on the corner of the bar.

'That's okay,' said George, 'I've got a phone; I'll just take the number.'

'Number doesn't work,' said the landlord.

George was sure she had seen a local taxi dropping someone off when they'd arrived, but she couldn't be bothered to argue, and was too sober to get into a fight.

They all stepped out into the sunset and searched on their phones for local taxi numbers. One by one, the search engines failed, and the phones failed, as they were miles from the nearest whisper of coverage.

And so they started a very long walk home, with only Timmy (who had been given some pasty scraps by the dog-loving Japanese) not looking tired and dejected . . .

CHAPTER TWELVE

A Cycling Adventure

'So what are you going to do today?' asked Aunt Fanny brightly of her guests, over the breakfast table next day.

They had all enjoyed a pleasant breakfast of black tea and porridge (made with gluten-free oats and nut milk) sprinkled with açai berries and bee pollen. This was accompanied by a new health-drink that was a spin on Anne's previous 'magic water'. It contained blended cold green tea, lime juice, mint leaves, cider vinegar, coconut milk and fresh ginger, and looked like it had been wrung out of a tramp's trousers. Anne had dubbed it 'sacred essence'.

Descending to the table, Uncle Quentin had eyed their break-fast bowls with a flared nostril before munching through a full English with enormous relish, simultaneously completing the *New Scientist* cryptic crossword with many dismissive tuts and sighs. Finishing his meal, he burped enormously and departed without a word, whistling as he climbed the stairs.

'Well, to answer your question, we'll go on an adventure. There's no shortage of coves and hills and cliffs and castles . . .'

It was decided at length that they would go on a cycle ride.

Julian took out his map and planned the route, tracing it in pencil. They would go for a long twenty-five-mile ride and get back in time for dinner, for which they would pick up ingredients on the way. The others thought twenty-five miles sounded a tad much, but agreed to it nonetheless.

'And perhaps you'll take with you some nice peanut-butter sandwiches for lunch!' said Aunt Fanny.

'We've discussed this, Mummy,' said George, putting a hand on her mother's arm. 'Why do you keep trying to force peanut butter on us?'

'It's all these blasted peanuts Quentin bought for this car of his,' said Aunt Fanny, looking despondent. 'We still have a quarter of a *tonne* left, piled in the old ice house. How we'll ever get rid of them . . .'

There was a pile of old bikes jumbled up in the one of the sheds behind Kirrin Cottage. On close inspection, it was established that there were indeed four that (after some oiling and pumping of tyres) were in good enough condition to ride.

While Dick was checking the bikes were good to go, Aunt Fanny prepared the picnic with Anne's help. Anne had taken the precaution of getting up early and asking Aunt Fanny to zap her into town so she could go to the twenty-four-hour Asda and get ingredients. And, truth be told, from the moment she had returned home, Anne had, in fact, been preparing their lunch.

She tried to hide from the others what an inordinate faff these meals were to make, but today's had been faffier than ever. She had managed to escape Aunt Fanny witnessing the first wave of excessive preparation, as she had spent the morning out with friends.

First, Anne had made a batch of nut milk (with which she had prepared their porridge). Then, for the next hour, she made everyone's breakfast, which, clattering downstairs in a disorderly fashion, as they did, they assumed had taken her no more than fifteen minutes. This, she was content for them to assume.

After eating her own breakfast, she assembled, peeled and chopped the ingredients for their lunch smoothie. By this time, Aunt Fanny had returned and was watching with polite detached interest.

'The key to these smoothies is to avoid too much fruit,' Anne explained to Aunt Fanny. 'Fruit is almost all sugar, no good for the body. It might as well be cocaine. A teaspoon of goji berries, cranberries and blueberries won't harm. They make the smoothie more palatable, in fact,' she conceded.

Aunt Fanny nodded, with the focused seriousness of

As usual, Timmy hunted around the table, waiting for scraps. Today, he hit the jackpot. At each chair he found handfuls of spiralized squash.

someone attending a ritual of an alien religion, which might easily turn out benevolent or diabolical.

Anne counted out the next four ingredients on her fingers. 'Ginger. Kale. Broccoli. Spinach. As Julian would say, they're your four attackers. All anti-inflammatory, all antioxidants. They also give you bone health, reduced cancer risk and provide gastrointestinal relief.' Anne stopped, as though to allow Aunt Fanny to draw breath, or give applause. She certainly looked startled.

'Next: chia seeds, brazil nut, carrot, beetroot . . .'

'Oh, Anne,' said Aunt Fanny, 'not beetroot. Not in a drink.'

'Hemp seeds,' Anne went on, 'pumpkin seeds, walnut and a teaspoon of resistant potato starch.'

'What would lunch be,' murmured Aunt Fanny, 'without resistant potato starch?'

'It's good for the gut. Helps you feel fuller, helps it work better and absorb more nutrients. You see, Aunt Fanny? I've got their best interests at heart. A glass of this for lunch is *very good for you*. The sort of thing that lovely Gwyneth Paltrow makes.'

'I've never been very keen on her,' said Aunt Fanny. 'There seems something so forced—'

Anne switched on the blender at the highest speed.

*

With everything ready and lunch packed, they set off well before eleven, and wound down the country roads through the hazy sunshine, ringing their bells with glee as Timmy trotted happily alongside. The beautiful landscape around them they glimpsed over hedgerows, and the twittering of the birds and the lowing cattle were just about audible above their aggressively rumbling stomachs. Hardly a car passed, and Anne started to believe this holiday might prove a chance to really cleanse themselves in another way: to escape the influence of technology, email and phone calls. All the mess of modern life!

As she crested a hill, Anne gazed up into the blue sky scattered with white wisps of cloud and took in a deep breath of fresh air. 'Isn't this *wonderful*?' she called over her shoulder.

Not hearing a reply, she braked to a halt and turned. She was surprised to find the other three were still far behind, only halfway up the hill. Their faces were grey and drawn, and Dick and Julian were clearly struggling with the effort. George had got off and was walking her bike; the two boys were puffing desperately.

'Come on, you lot!' Anne shouted cheerfully. None of them even looked at her.

It took a surprisingly long time for the others to reach the top of the hill, and when they did, the sky had clouded over somewhat. But it still offered a wonderful view.

'Not Kirrin Island, but it's still marvellous, isn't it?' Anne asked. The others couldn't answer because they were panting too hard. She consulted the map while they were getting their breath back. 'You're out of shape,' she said reprovingly, and added, 'Well, at least this next stretch is the easy bit.' Then, pushing herself off again, she freewheeled to the bottom of the hill.

Considering the bearing and condition of her fellow adventurers, Anne decided that an early lunch was called for. After that, she was sure, the others would be back to their normal selves and have the wind in their sails, and the trip would unfold with the usual energy and happiness that had always marked their time together.

She stopped at a sunny spot on the side of a hill that offered a pretty view over the harbour. The others flopped on to the grass around her as Anne laid out the picnic blanket and unpacked the lunch from her panniers.

'Now, I've got some pretty exciting treats lined up,' she said. 'So I hope you're hungry.' She wished she hadn't made that last remark as soon as it was out of her mouth. Despite being bent over the picnic hamper, she felt the cold stares of the others drill into her back. Although it was a very warm day, the sensation gave her goose bumps.

First, she poured some dry food out for Timmy, but, despite

73

her placing it directly in front of him, and its being in his usual food bowl, he did not even look at it, and instead bounded into the bushes to expend some of his last remaining energy on trying to catch something with a pulse. 'Dear old Timmy,' she muttered, laughing.

Then she got out the large container that held the smoothie she had prepared for lunch, and poured it into four plastic cups, handing them round. George took hers politely, Dick with some trepidation and Julian with stoic indifference.

'Now, this is terribly good for you,' said Anne. 'In so many ways. It boosts your immune system, helps your kidneys and your liver, gives long-lasti— Julian? Where has yours gone?'

'Drank it,' said Julian. His gaze had not moved from the middle distance since he sat down. He was not licking his lips or wiping his mouth or swallowing, or any of the things that people generally do when they've drunk a cup of something the moment before. His posture was, in fact, entirely unaltered from when she had handed him the cup. Except that the cup was now empty.

'Did you?' she asked.

'Yes,' he said simply.

Anne had never before in her entire life had recourse to accuse Julian of lying. In fact, to do so was not in her power. Yet she was now aware, in a calm, objective way, that Julian

They thought about how much weight they must have lost already – it had been over a week now, after all – and wondered if they had earned something like a burger and chips.

had not drunk that drink. She could not prove it, and there was nothing to be achieved by trying.

She turned back to the others and continued to expound on the virtues of the smoothie she had prepared, and her reasons for each ingredient. She mentioned the high omega-3 content in chia seeds, and Dick nodded. She talked about the high zinc content in pumpkin seeds, and George smiled. They both seemed to be impressed when she told them that hemp seeds contained all twenty amino acids.

Dick decided to be first to try the drink.

He held it up in front of himself rather gingerly, as though he were a scientist and this was the result of a dangerous experiment.

'Oh, Dick, you make such a big deal out of things. Just swallow it down! I know it's a funny colour, but it tastes just fine, I promise.'

She was not wrong about the drink's unappetizing appearance. It had a sludgy consistency and was the colour of orange juice mixed with horse manure. As the mixture touched his lips, Dick closed his eyes and winced. He took a sip and his eyes bulged. He clapped a hand over his mouth and, with difficulty, contained several internal explosions. When the urge to vomit had been suppressed, he removed his hand, letting out a long, ragged breath and wiping a tear from his eye.

George and Julian watched with open enjoyment. This was the first good distraction they had had for a while from their own hunger and discomfort.

Glancing at his sister, and deciding to get this over with once and for all, Dick pinched his nose with one hand and then poured the drink in, gulping unpleasantly, eyes screwed shut, until it was all gone. Then he lay the cup to one side, panting, and wiped his mouth.

George and Julian broke into wild applause. It was the most fun they had enjoyed in weeks.

Meanwhile, Anne sipped from her own cup (it really did make you feel alive to drink it – she could almost feel the weight melting off her with each sip – no matter what the others thought) and looked out to sea, relaxing and letting the coastal breeze wash over her.

CHAPTER THIRTEEN

Things Come to a Head

'Now,' said Anne, her recent suspicions forgotten and all her old cheerfulness back in force, 'it's time for the main course.'

To everyone's astonishment, she proceeded to remove from the picnic basket her spiralizer, which she laid out on the picnic blanket, along with a variety of vegetables. They could not contain themselves, and a groan rose up from around the camp.

Anne was shocked at this sudden open rebellion, and gazed round at them. Dick and Julian looked somewhat abashed at what had clearly been an involuntary reaction to the sight of the dreaded machine.

George, however, still looked quite cheerful.

'Oh, I say,' she chirruped, 'was that Timmy barking? I'd better go and look for him.' No one had heard the slightest peep out of Timmy, but nevertheless George jumped up and disappeared into the bushes.

'I'm sorry, dear Anne,' said Julian. 'I didn't mean to sound so ungrateful. But I feel as though I haven't eaten a real meal in years. I don't feel better, I just feel empty and hungry. I don't think I can bear another serving of fresh vegetables smeared with healthy goo.'

'It's a delicious recipe,' Anne said. 'Courgette noodles and broad bean salad, with a soy dressing. Nutritious and filling!'

She looked at Dick, who was still feeling shaky from his downing of the slurry smoothie a few moments before.

'I don't know, Anne,' he said. 'I don't know . . .'

'But what can you possibly be unsure about? Does that smoothie not make you feel better?'

'It does, it does,' he admitted. 'In a manner of speaking. But there's something about all this that just makes me feel as though I'm not *living*.'

'Not living?'

'Not really,' Dick said. 'I'm doing all the things that people who are alive do, except the ones I like.'

'To be honest, on this diet, I feel grey,' admitted Julian. 'Like I'm watching myself on a screen.'

Anne goggled at them both, aware that half the temper that was rising in her came from her deep suspicion, deep down, despite her fervent promotion of this cause, that she had been feeling these exact same things herself all along. Except she had managed to squeeze and crush those feelings down until they were gone. Why couldn't everyone do that?

'We can't stop *now*,' she said. 'We've hardly started! That's not the spirit we enter into things with!'

'With which we enter into things,' said Julian quietly.

'Anyway,' said Anne, 'everyone says the first few weeks are the hardest. After that, you'll never look back.'

The boys both looked chastised and refused to meet her eye.

Anne stood, hands on hips. 'Okay,' she said. 'I'll ask George if she feels the same way. If she does, we'll give up the diet and go back to our bad old ways.'

The boys didn't seem happy with themselves at having driven their sister to this desperate bargain. They nodded miserably as she set off into the bushes along the hilltop to try and find George and Timmy.

Ordinarily, Anne would have called out, but she was feeling so upset and confused that, as she walked along, she found herself debating aloud whether she had been right or wrong to try and foist this diet upon the others. She had done it for their own good. And it was, undoubtedly, healthy. But it was no good if the diet made her brothers feel grey, and dead inside. In fact, all this mindfulness business was supposed to have precisely the opposite effect . . . It was all so confusing!

Anne went along, muttering to herself like a mad woman,

'It's just, when I've eaten three of your healthy meals on the trot, I really feel like I've earned some proper food, you know?'

only startled out of her introversion when she broke through a gap in the bushes and came across a terrible sight.

She put her hands to her mouth and screamed.

The boys came running, darting into the clearing in a matter of seconds, ready for action. When all they discovered was Anne and George sitting on the ground and Timmy sniffing a thistle, they felt a slight anticlimax. Short of energy as they were, they leant on each other's shoulders to catch their breath, and asked what was going on.

Anne just pointed at George, who was still brushing crumbs off her trousers. She was red-faced with shame.

'We thought you were being kidnapped,' said Julian. 'By pirates or spies.'

'Or thieves,' said Dick. 'Or escaped lunatics or murderers. What's wrong?'

Anne just pointed.

'George, would you mind explaining, rather than us waiting for Anne to recover the power of speech?' asked Julian.

'Fine,' said George, standing, as Timmy bounced happily around her. 'She caught me eating some illicit items. Some . . . contraband.'

'*George*,' said Dick. 'You mean you deliberately *smuggled*?'

'Smugglers!' said Julian. 'That's the other group I was going to say we thought you were being kidnapped by. Pirates, spies or *smugglers*. How could I forget them?'

'But, George, that makes you no better than the ruffians we used to catch at their dirty games!'

'Oh, *come* on,' said George. 'I only hid a slice of bloody cake in my shirt. I wasn't selling the crown jewels to Soviets, or something.'

Sat on the ground next to her, Anne looked disconsolate. George couldn't bear to see her this way.

'*Dear* Anne,' she said, putting her arm round her. 'I've followed our diet *almost* all the time. For two weeks, I haven't so much as looked at a cheese sandwich. It's just, when I've eaten three of your healthy meals on the trot, I really feel like I've earned some *proper* food, you know? I mean, don't we all feel that way? Haven't we all secretly sneaked in some unhealthy snacks because we think we've earned them?'

Julian and Dick both failed to meet George's eye. And, when she looked at Anne, even she could not truly say she had remained pure.

'I ate a packet of Wotsits,' Anne said at last. 'I'm not proud of myself. I felt so sinful. And they didn't even taste of real cheese!' Anne buried her head in her hands and wept. The others didn't feel this was worth crying about, so started walking back to the picnic area.

'Buck up, dear girl,' said Julian. 'We won't get through life if we cry over Wotsits, now, will we?'

'Yes, that's true; thanks, Julian,' said Anne. 'But, George, you also led Timmy astray.'

'He's an old dog,' said George, 'and he's *my* old dog. I don't see why he should be forced to undergo some fashionable human diet during his declining years. So I smuggled him out some sausages.'

'Woof!' said Timmy loudly, approving heartily of the word 'sausages'.

'Oh, I wasn't really trying to make *him* go through our diet,' said Anne. 'I was just trying to get him on to a regular dog's diet. And to stop you feeding him sausages.'

'Woof!' said Timmy again.

'They're not good for dogs, you see,' said Anne. 'His stomach can't handle them. And they make him fart terribly.'

'Ah,' George said, nodding with realization, while Timmy licked her face enthusiastically. At that moment, a familiar and unpleasant smell washed over the group, and George realized that, in one important respect, at least, Anne had been right all along.

CHAPTER FOURTEEN

The Ride Home Is Interrupted

Julian, George and Dick all felt beastly about the way they had acted, and so, when they came back to the picnic, they ate the courgette noodles and broad bean salad with many loud utterances of approval. Then they helped Anne pack up the picnic, consulted Julian's map together, and set out on their bikes once more, with Timmy trotting along behind. After their heart-to-heart, they felt more like a group than they had for months.

However, they all knew the concept of their diet had suffered a crucial blow from which it could not recover, and they all secretly wondered how much longer the pretence could last. It would last, the other three knew, as long as Anne's stubbornness would hold out, a quality which had always proven remarkably durable, and had never yet been known to yield.

As they cycled for mile after mile down sunny lanes, they all pondered the topic and hardly dared hope she would drop it. Anne, meanwhile, was battling with a larger thought that was entirely more troubling: that she had introduced something

*They had all enjoyed their breakfast of black tea and
porridge (made with gluten-free oats and nut milk)
sprinkled with açai berries and bee pollen.*

into this group that had tested it, and found it wanting. In all previous adventures, they had never faced failure like this – and Anne had brought it about. Perhaps that was what adult life was, Anne wondered with a shock: getting used to things not being precisely as you hoped. It was with sobering reflections such as these that Anne and the others cycled in silence, through the afternoon heat . . .

One way or another, they were all so thoroughly distracted that, after a good while, they suddenly realized they had been travelling for miles down a stretch of road that bore no relation to their route on the map. Losing their way was not something they would normally do as a group under any circumstances, and, after looking again at the map, they refused to believe they had gone wrong. So they decided it must be the map that was in error.

After consulting and once more dismissing the map a while later, they kept cycling in a defiantly cheery mood for a good way before it became impossible to ignore. They were lost.

'Google Maps is no use out here either,' said Dick, pocketing his phone.

They heard a motor approaching from over the hill, and then a van appeared, which they waved down.

'I say,' said Dick, 'I'm terribly sorry, but w—'

'It's YOU!' yelled the driver. 'Well I never!'

All four of them flinched.

'Is it?' asked Dick.

'What do you mean, it's us?' asked George. 'What is?'

The driver was a plump, cheerful man in his forties. He looked to be driving a delivery van for a living, and yet for some reason he was clearly ecstatic to have run into the four (or five) of them.

'Oh, they'll never believe it,' he chuckled. 'Are you out here enjoying the sunshine, then? Going for a nice bike ride?'

They told him that that was exactly what they were doing, except they had lost their way.

'Oh HO!' he said. 'I'll show you the way back to civilization. Only there's one very small favour I'll ask.'

'Anything,' said George. 'We'd be delighted.'

'Stick your bikes in the back of the van, then, because we're going to stop by my kids' school,' said the man. 'It's their annual prize-giving.'

This sounded like a perfectly acceptable trade, and so they piled their bikes next to each other in the back of the van and found places to sit comfortably while it bounced over the hills, creaking noisily from every direction. For Julian and Dick, this was an ideal solution, as the courgette noodles had made few inroads into their hunger and the ten- or fifteen-mile journey home had seemed like a bitter prospect, no matter the beauty of the surroundings. As the van bumped along, George tried to get some sense of why they would be invited to a school prize-giving.

'I don't know why *we* would be so interesting . . .' she said over the driver's shoulder.

'You're havin' a laugh, ain'tcha?' asked the driver.

'I wish people would stop asking us that,' said Dick. 'I'm never "having a laugh", as far as I'm aware.'

'Fancy having you lot in the back of me van,' the driver chuckled. 'Why, you lot are famous around these parts; didn't you know that?'

'Maybe you've mistaken us for some other people . . .' piped up Anne. She was going to follow this by suggesting some other four-strong group of young people with a dog who might possibly be well known in this part of Dorset, but her imagination failed her. Perhaps they resembled some exciting new band on the hit parade, who had got lost on a tour of Hardy's Wessex – but surely no music group could possibly dress as they did. Perhaps, after all, it *was* the four (or five) of them that the man was delighted to meet, but she couldn't for the life of her fathom why.

As he raced around corners far too quick, the driver couldn't stop chuckling. 'Why, fancy you not knowing how well known you is,' he said. 'Fancy that!'

Suddenly, they were all heaved in the air and then squished up together as the van crested a speed bump at maximum velocity and braked to a halt. A moment later, the van's side door was hauled back on its rollers with a thunderous noise. Clambering out, they found themselves in front of an old Victorian school building. Timmy yelped with happiness and zipped off into the distance, chasing after some delicious odour.

'They won't believe it,' said the driver, still chuckling to himself as he walked away to find someone in reception.

CHAPTER FIFTEEN

Extra-Special Guests

Julian, Dick, Anne and George stretched their limbs for a moment in the sun, then clambered back into the van to retrieve their bicycles. They would have looked for somewhere secure to place them (they wondered, for a moment, if schools still had bike sheds, these days), but this school seemed to be about half a mile from the nearest habitation, and, what's more, the bikes they were riding had probably looked rusty and out of date about thirty-five years ago. The idea of someone stealing them seemed positively fanciful, so they just leant them together against the gate.

'What does he mean, we're well known?' asked Dick. 'It doesn't stand to reason.'

'He does also use rather a large number of clichés, but who am I to argue?' asked Anne. 'He gave us a lift in our hour of need.'

'Cor, strike a light and no mistake!' yelled a familiar voice. 'Here they are, and no word of a lie, as I live and breathe.'

Their driver had reappeared alongside a very agitated

middle-aged lady who had a great deal of curly russet hair and wore a pair of spectacles, which she peered through and then over, one after the other, again and again, for several moments. She had the air of a woman who had long ago got used to the feeling of being highly stressed, but who nonetheless was, at this moment, quite unusually (by her standards) stressed.

'You are Julian, George, Dick and Anne?' she asked.

They nodded.

She had a thought. 'And Timmy, I believe, ran past me in the corridor?'

'Woof!' agreed Timmy, who, having concluded his preliminary investigation of the grounds, had returned. This made the woman jump.

'Yes, good. It's so nice of you to come, and such good timing. I am Mrs Pleasance, the headmistress of this multi-faith school. Please come with me.' She turned and vanished back in through a side door in the school's rather grand main building before they had had a chance to express their astonishment that she knew of them (or, more amazingly, Timmy), and their pleasure at being made so welcome. They tried to keep up as she hurried through empty classrooms made dark by the bright sunshine outside.

'We had a local children's author booked, but he never showed,' Mrs Pleasance said fretfully, over her shoulder. 'I

'I'm sorry, dear Anne,' said Julian. 'I didn't mean to sound ungrateful but I feel as though I haven't eaten a real meal for years.'

was warned he might be no good. Heard on the grapevine he's a bit of a . . .' She stopped and turned, miming the 'drinky-drinky' motion.

'How do you know of us?' asked George, but Mrs Pleasance had vanished through a door into a blanket of bright sunshine.

George held Timmy back, because she saw that the door gave on to some grass that quickly sloped away. She sensed that the main sports field was below, and, if this was a prize-giving, that was where people would be gathered, looking up. She inched out of the door, into a group of adults all standing up straight and facing outwards. The others followed her, somewhat uncertainly.

There was the sharpening whine of a microphone being adjusted, which they heard echo out loudly from speakers a long way apart.

'Now,' said the voice of the headmistress, 'at the last moment, we are very lucky to be joined by some extra-special guests. This really is a treat. They just happened to be in the neighbourhood and, when they realized we were without a speaker, they kindly agreed to come and speak to you on this special day,' Mrs Pleasance went on.

George, Julian, Dick and Anne were squeezing between the tight press of teachers, towards where the woman was standing, and trying (despite the crush) to shoot each other quizzical looks. What on earth was this woman talking about? The four of them (with Timmy in tow) at last stumbled into the space by the podium as Mrs Pleasance began her full introduction.

'Now, children, you know the stories I've told you about a group of heroic youths, just like you, who had the strength of will and sense of purpose to defeat smugglers and spies and thieves? Julian, George, Dick, Anne and Timmy the dog? Well, here they are!'

The four of them now had a good view down the slope and out over the sports field, where several hundred children and a similar number of parents were assembled, all looking up expectantly at them. Clearly, it was a special day for the school, for a large marquee had been erected over part of the pitch. As the audience caught sight of the five of them, to their bewildered surprise, it broke into applause. They could not understand how this applause could possibly be for them.

'We've often told stories of your exploits,' the headmistress explained. The five of them just looked confused. 'We've heard tales of your heroism, you see, and we've told them to children for years and years. Thousands and thousands of children have learnt by your example.'

'I'm sure it was exaggerated,' said Dick.

'What was?' asked Mrs Pleasance.

'Whatever you heard,' said Dick.

'And they're modest too,' said Mrs Pleasance, to the group's acute embarrassment.

'So, now we at last have the chance to ask you in person,' Mrs Pleasance went on, turning towards the group, 'what qualities do *you* think are important for young people to grow up good and strong, and happy and healthy, and to possibly achieve acts of heroism like yours?'

With this, she took the microphone off the stand and held it beneath Dick's nose. Dick coughed modestly, a cough which was amplified through the loud speakers at either end of the field and rippled over the crowd's heads.

What Mrs Pleasance didn't understand was that the very terms of the question went entirely against the ethos of their little group. They never acted in any way they thought of as heroic, only in the way that felt right. They were just themselves, and they instinctively found the idea of being idolized in any way, or being famous – if that was what they were – to be entirely alarming. In short, there was no answer to the question.

On top of which, Dick was not really a 'big questions' kind of guy. He just liked to get on with things. Plus, he had never spoken in front of a crowd before, and had been given no time to think of an answer.

*'The key to making smoothies is to avoid too much fruit.
Fruit is almost all sugar. It might as well be cocaine.'*

'Er,' he said, looking desperately at Julian. But, instead, it was Anne who took the microphone.

'Why, thank you for asking,' she said smoothly. 'It's most incredibly lovely to be here at St Gertrude's, and may I say everyone looks wonderful this afternoon. To answer your question, the truth is we had no idea that anyone ever knew of our little adventures – no idea at all. And, if anything, the news makes us (such as Dick, here) rather bashful. But, if you want to know the quality we have always lived and sworn by,' she continued, looking round at George and Julian, who openly gaped at this new, sophisticated Anne who was appearing in front of them, 'well, that is sticking together, and not letting each other down, no matter what.

'When we set out to do a thing,' she went on, 'we do it. And, by jingo, we do it as a *group*. We don't let anything stand in our way. Not tiredness, nor hunger, nor the temptation to give up. Because, after all, friendship is stronger than *anything*. Isn't it?' She finished this peroration by throwing out her arm and inviting the others to agree. As tired and vexed as they were, they found themselves overcome with emotion at this fervent outburst, and could not help but agree wholeheartedly. She had spoken the truth, after all – and suddenly their friendship was whole again. Stronger than ever, in fact. It had survived another test. The three of them broke out in applause, and the crowd followed suit.

'Woof!' said Timmy enthusiastically. 'Woof, woof!'

'Stirring words from Anne, there,' said Mrs Pleasance, as Anne wriggled back between Dick and Julian, giving each of them a big hug. 'Now, I'm sure our special guests will be delighted to be the judges of the big school bake-off in the large tent . . .'

*

At first, they thought they had misheard her. But, with the sensation of being mere pawns of fate, the five of them were swept down the hill by the surge of the crowd, and soon enough were deposited in a large marquee.

'The children have been practising baking all term,' beamed the headmistress, gesturing towards two large trestle tables. These extended the entire length of the marquee – perhaps thirty feet – and along their entire lengths were placed enough baked goods to feed an army. They were divided into sections: biscuits, cakes, breads, buns, quiches, pies and tarts. Each had been thoughtfully dissected into equal pieces for the judges all to taste. What's more, it seemed that, beyond its multi-faith remit, this was also a school for the gifted, or some hothouse for junior culinary talent, because all the food looked utterly amazing.

The four friends and Timmy stood there, so lately apprised of their fame, surrounded on every side by the sort of feast they had all been dreaming of for weeks, and with Anne's words still ringing in their ears. Hunger and emotions boiled inside them. Dick put a finger to his bottom lip just in time to prevent a line of drool descending from it.

It was too much for them to handle. Looking down at the perfectly turned out cheese twists and croissants and vol-au-vents and flans, Julian plucked up a slice of one of the tastiest-looking flans and raised it to his opened mouth, just as the microphone was placed in front of Anne.

She didn't think. She just screamed at the top of her voice: '*Juuuuuuuuuuuuuuuuu!*'

CHAPTER SIXTEEN

A Brisk Journey Home

'Come along now, faster!' Anne called, pedalling hard.

Julian came up on the inside and took the lead. He had dropped the physical map half a mile ago as he tried to consult it while accelerating at full pelt. Now he was risking his smartphone by trying to consult Google Maps on that.

'How funny that they should have heard of us!' said Dick, catching up.

'Yes, I think the stories they tell about us will be considerably different from now on, don't you, Anne?' asked George.

'Woof!' agreed Timmy regretfully.

'I thought we agreed not to talk about it,' said Anne, over her shoulder.

'Now that they think we're racists,' George said.

'Not talking about it!' squeaked Anne, pedalling faster than ever.

'Pity we don't have Quentin's peanut car to hand,' said Julian.

She thought of Gwyneth Paltrow, so clean and happy and pure.

'Oh, he told me this morning he's ditching it,' said George. 'Turns out running a car literally on peanuts is, in fact, prohibitively expensive.'

'Jolly lucky we left our bikes by the entrance, then,' said Dick.

'I can't tell which road we need to take at this next turning ...' called Julian, his bike wobbling slightly as he looked at his phone.

'We're all right now,' said George. 'I started recognizing these roads a while ago. Straight ahead, everyone!'

The energy and excitement of their sudden exit had caused them all to forget the woes of their stomachs for the time being. After her little faux pas, Anne had vehemently ordered the others to leave with her as fast as possible, fearing a misunderstanding was about to develop that words were powerless to resolve.

'They probably knew what I really meant by it *really*,' Anne said for the seventh time. 'Or, at least, they'll work it out. They know Julian's name, after all.'

'Yes, they do,' said Julian, letting go his handlebars and resting back on his seat as they all crested a hill and entered a downhill stretch. 'But I can't help feeling we were well advised to leave at that juncture.'

Cruising downhill, they all eased off on the pedalling for the first time in three miles. They began cautiously to feel safe from the lynch mob they had expected to be coming to kill them – or, worse, coming to drag them back to explain themselves. But it seemed, at last, that risk had passed.

'Thank God none of us is on Twitter,' said George. 'Tell me, Anne, how do you feel about the diet now?'

'Well,' said Anne, 'I think, overall, it's brought us closer together. This is the first real adventure we've had for years.'

'Agreed,' said George.

Dick and Julian weaved in and out of each other on their

bikes, refusing to pass comment. They didn't disagree, but they wanted Anne to follow her own train of thought.

This she did, as she watched the sun setting over the black-berry bushes in the westerly hedgerow. She thought about that nice Gwyneth Paltrow, what a wonderful life she seemed to live, so clean and happy and pure. And, all the while, mindfully, she observed her own thoughts.

Anne looked over all they had been through so far, as they followed the diet, and what it would be like to continue with it for the rest of their lives. She looked at her dear companions, who had come through so much with her over the years. Seeing that they were approaching a bridge, she reached back into one of her panniers, unbuckled it, and managed to grab hold of the spiralizer.

'Yeah,' she said. 'It's all a load of . . .'

Dick's breath caught in his throat. He had never heard Anne utter so much as the mildest profanity in all his life. 'A load of . . . *power balls*?' he suggested.

'I was going to say, it's all a load of bollocks, isn't it?' Anne said, heaving the spiralizer, with all her might, over the wall and into the river below. 'Race you home!' And, bending over the bars, she pedalled like mad until she was far out in front.

Timmy liked nothing better than a race and, yelping heartily, he threw himself into it, sure that he would win!

'There's something about all this that just makes me feel as though I'm not **living**. I'm doing all the things that people who are alive do, except the ones I like.'